Hairy Maclary Scattercat

Lynley Dodd

PUFFIN

Hairy Maclary
felt bumptious and bustly,
bossy and bouncy
and frisky and hustly.
He wanted to run.
He wanted to race.
But the MAIN thing he wanted
was something
to
chase.

Greywacke Jones
was hunting a bee.

BUT ALONG CAME HAIRY MACLARY. . .

and chased her up high
in the sycamore tree.

Butterball Brown
was washing a paw.

BUT ALONG CAME HAIRY MACLARY. . .

and bustled him under
a rickety door.

Pimpernel Pugh
was patting a ball.

BUT ALONG CAME HAIRY MACLARY. . .

and chased her away
over Pemberton's wall.

Slinky Malinki
was down in the reeds.

BUT ALONG CAME HAIRY MACLARY. . .

and hustled him into
a drum full of weeds.

Mushroom Magee
was asleep on a ledge.

BUT ALONG CAME HAIRY MACLARY. . .

and chased her away
through a hole in the hedge.

Down on the path
by an old wooden rail,
twitching a bit,
was the tip of a tail.
With a bellicose bark
and a boisterous bounce,
Hairy Maclary
was ready
to
POUNCE

BUT AROUND CAME SCARFACE CLAW. . .

who bothered
and bustled him,
rustled and hustled him,
raced him
and chased him

ALL the way
home.

PUFFIN BOOKS
Published by the Penguin Group: London, New York, Australia, Canada, India, Ireland, New Zealand and South Africa
Penguin Books Ltd, Registered Offices: 80 Strand, London WC2R 0RL, England

puffinbooks.com

First published in New Zealand by Mallinson Rendel Publishers Ltd 1985
First published in Great Britain in Puffin Books 1987
Reissued in 2005
This edition published 2007
4
Text and illustrations copyright © Lynley Dodd, 1985
All rights reserved
The moral right of the author/illustrator has been asserted
Made and printed in China
ISBN: 978-1-85613-081-3
This edition produced for The Book People Ltd, Hall Wood Avenue, Haydock, St Helens, WA11 9UL